mermaids
ROCK
The Midnight Realm

To Luca, Lara, Milly, Alfie, and Erin—cool cousins,
always ready for an adventure—L.C.

To my grandma, who kept buying tiny notebooks
for me to doodle in—M.O.

tiger tales

5 River Road, Suite 128, Wilton, CT 06897
Published in the United States 2022
Originally published in Great Britain 2021
by the Little Tiger Group
Text copyright © 2021 Linda Chapman
Illustrations copyright © 2021 Mirelle Ortega
ISBN-13: 978-1-6643-4002-2
ISBN-10: 1-6643-4002-5
Printed in China
STP/1800/0430/1021
2 4 6 8 10 9 7 5 3 1

www.tigertalesbooks.com

MERMAIDS ROCK

The Midnight Realm

by Linda Chapman
Illustrated by Mirelle Ortega

tiger tales

Contents

Welcome to Mermaids Rock!

Marina & Sammy

Kai & Tommy

Naya &
Octavia

Coralie & Dash

Luna &
Melly

Chapter One
An Exciting Announcement

"Our project is looking great!" said Naya, admiring the poster about coral that she and her best friends were working on. They'd been making it for a couple of weeks now, and Naya was really proud of what they'd done. They had been able to combine all of their skills! Coralie and Kai, who were the best at art, had drawn pictures of different types of coral, and Marina and Naya had written out a bunch of information. Luna, Coralie's younger cousin, had designed the poster, doing a big heading in bubble writing and sticking everything on.

"When we add our secret *you-know-whats*, it will look even more *clam-tastic*!" said Coralie with a swish of her purple tail.

Naya felt a rush of excitement. Everyone's projects looked good, but she hoped theirs would win.

"I wonder what the prize will be…," said Kai, the only merboy in their group. He had dark hair and a red tail. "I hope it's going to be something exciting like a day off from school or a huge clamshell filled with candy!"

"I wouldn't worry about the prize, Kai Stormchaser," said Glenda, giving him a snooty look over her shoulder. She sat in front with her friends, Jazeela and Racquel. "There's no way you're going to win this competition. Our poster is much better than yours. Look!"

She swam back to reveal the almost-finished project her group was working on. "My dad visited tons of different places through the magic whirlpool and got us some coral from each one to stick on to our poster. We don't just have boring drawings—we have the actual coral itself."

Naya frowned. "But we're not supposed to collect coral. It takes thousands of years for a reef to form, and each coral only grows a tiny amount every year."

Glenda rolled her eyes. "Of course my dad didn't break the coral off! He found the broken pieces on the seabed."

"But this is a project we're supposed to do by ourselves," Naya protested. "Your dad shouldn't have helped you. It's wrong."

"You're just jealous." Glenda tossed her long blond hair. "Get ready for us to win!"

Marina put her hands on her hips. "I wouldn't be so sure about that, Glenda Seaglass."

4

Just then Ms. Sylvie, their teacher, clapped her hands. "Okay, everyone. Please, can you look this way? I have an exciting announcement to make." With a flick of her silvery tail, she swam to the front of the classroom and waited for everyone's full attention.

Naya put the top on her squid-ink pen and laid it down on the desk, lining it up neatly with her other pens. What was Ms. Sylvie going to tell them?

"I wonder what this is about," Luna whispered from her seat beside Naya.

"I hope it's something fun. Maybe we're going to get to do some experiments or spend a whole week doing nothing but science projects!" Naya whispered back.

Everyone fell quiet.

"As you know, it is vital that you learn about coral," Ms. Sylvie began. "When you're older, you will be responsible for helping to protect the coral reefs, along with other marine environments—the kelp forests, the polar regions, the mangrove swamps, the deep sea."

Naya nodded. Merpeople had to take care of all the oceans. Some traveled around the world, helping wherever there were natural or man-made disasters. Others stayed on the remote tropical reef where the merpeople had their home. There they could join the merguard who protected the reef, work with sea creatures in the Marine Sanctuary, or become teachers or scientists. When the merchildren were twelve, they went to a different school, where they could learn more about these jobs. Naya's dream was to become either an inventor or a research scientist like Marina's dad, Tarak.

"Your projects on types of coral must be handed in on Monday morning," Ms. Sylvie continued. "After that, we will start to study the different types of coral reefs—platform reefs, barrier reefs, fringing reefs, atolls...."

Glenda rolled her eyes at Racquel and Jazeela. "I thought Ms. Sylvie said she was going to tell us something exciting."

Ms. Sylvie's gaze snapped in their direction. Naya sat up straight, hoping that Ms. Sylvie didn't think it had been her speaking. That was one of the worst things about having to sit behind Glenda in class. Not only was she mean, but sometimes she said things or messed around, and Naya and her friends got the blame because they sat near her. Glenda never owned up when they got into trouble— she was *so* annoying!

Ms. Sylvie frowned at them for a moment, but then she continued. "To help you develop a real understanding of reefs, I have decided it would be very useful to go on a field trip." A murmur of excitement ran around the class. "So next week we're going on a three-day excursion—we'll be camping on a deserted atoll in the South Pacific Ocean. What do you think about that?" Ms. Sylvie's smile spread into a broad grin as the murmur became a chorus of excited exclamations.

"Camping!"

"We're going to the South Pacific!"

"Oh, bubbles!"

"I wonder what sea creatures we'll see!" Luna said to Naya. She had a special knack

with animals whether they had fins, fur, or feathers. They always wanted to be her friend!

"I bet we'll see *tons* of different creatures. This is going to be amazing!" exclaimed Naya. There would be so much to see and learn in a new place. "I have some books on atolls. Did you know they usually form around the crater of an underwater volcano, and when the volcano erodes, all that's left is the reef? Most of them are found in the Pacific Ocean."

Glenda looked around. "Seriously? Could you be any more dull, Naya?"

"Nerdy Naya!" giggled Racquel. "As boring as a sea slug!"

Naya looked embarrassed.

"Ignore them, Naya," said Marina loyally. "You're right. Atolls are really fascinating. You can bring your books on the trip and tell us about them."

"We can also have midnight snacks!" said Coralie, her eyes gleaming.

"And tell ghost stories!" Kai chipped in.

"I've been to the South Pacific before. It's beautiful," said Marina. She had spent most of her life traveling all over the world with her dad. "It'll be great to go there on a trip!"

"*Reef-ly* great, in fact!" said Coralie. They all looked at her blankly. "*Reefly?* Instead of really," she said. "*Reefly* great—get it?"

Naya hit her forehead with her hands as they groaned. Coralie loved telling bad jokes!

Ms. Sylvie started speaking again. "Obviously you'll need to get permission from your parents. I also want to make it quite clear that anyone who misbehaves between now and then will not be coming. So best behavior, please! Now get going and finish your projects. I'll be grading them on Monday, and the prize for the group whose poster gets the highest mark will get first choice of a camping spot at the atoll—as well as a giant bag of peppermint candy!"

Luna put her hand up.

"Yes, Luna?"

"Can we bring our pets on the trip?" she asked hopefully. Several of the merchildren—including all of her friends—had sea creatures as pets.

Naya crossed her fingers, willing Ms. Sylvie to say yes. Octavia, her clever octopus, would love to come with them.

"Yes, you can," said Ms. Sylvie. She lifted her voice above the chorus of cheers. "Provided they're well behaved and well trained."

Kai poked Glenda in the back as everyone set to work. "Guess you won't be bringing Silver, that porpoise you entered in the talent contest," he said.

"Not unless you want to end up covered in cake!" Coralie giggled.

Glenda's face darkened. A few weeks ago, there had been a competition to find the most talented pet. Glenda had cheated by asking her dad to get her a highly trained guard porpoise. Unfortunately, she hadn't realized that these animals were only obedient when they had their special work harnesses on. She'd taken Silver, her porpoise, to the competition using only a leash of ribbon seaweed, and he had ignored all of her commands. Then he had towed her straight into the cake table, leaving her covered in frosting.

"It was a total *cake-tastrophe*!" Coralie said.

"Oh, ha ha," Glenda said sarcastically.

"You're about as funny as a sea jelly sting, Coralie Glittertail!"

Kai grinned. "You should wear frosting on your face more often, Glenda. It suits you!"

Glenda's eyes flashed with fury, and she reached out and knocked a pot of ink over. It spilled on the drawing of staghorn coral that Kai had been working on all during class. "Now who's laughing?" she said spitefully as the paint spread across the seaweed parchment.

"Glenda, that was horrible!" said Marina, outraged.

"You just ruined Kai's picture!" cried Naya.

"What's going on here?" Ms. Sylvie's voice cut across them.

Glenda gave the teacher her best *I'm-such-a-perfect-mergirl* look that grown-ups almost always fell for. "Oh, Ms. Sylvie, I'm *so* sorry," she said, putting her hand on her heart. "I just turned around to ask Kai if I could borrow a pen, and I accidentally knocked the ink over. I am really, *really* sorry," she said. "Now Kai will have to do his picture all over again. I do feel terrible."

Naya and the others glared at her, but Glenda just blinked back at them as if it actually had been an accident. None of the five friends ever liked to snitch, so they didn't tell Ms. Sylvie the truth.

"Oh, dear, what a shame," said Ms. Sylvie, shaking her head. "Well, accidents do happen.

I'm afraid you'll have to start your picture again, Kai, or leave it out of your project."

"I'll do it again," sighed Kai, reaching for a new piece of parchment.

Ms. Sylvie turned to swim back to the front of the class.

Naya and her friends leaned forward to hiss angry words at Glenda, but as they did, Glenda picked up her paintbrush and jerked it violently, leaving a big black smudge over the bottom of her picture. "Ms. Sylvie!" she squealed. "Kai and Coralie just messed up my painting! Look what they've done! They're so mean!"

Chapter Two
In Trouble

"Kai! Coralie!" Ms. Sylvie exclaimed as she saw the big, black smudge. "What made you do something like that to Glenda's work?"

"We didn't!" spluttered Kai.

"It was Glenda!" exclaimed Coralie. "She did it herself!"

"She did," Marina protested. Naya and Luna nodded.

"They're lying!" cried Glenda. "Why would I ruin my own painting, Ms. Sylvie? I just picked up my brush, and they knocked my arm on purpose to get back at me for *accidentally* spilling ink on Kai's picture."

Ms. Sylvie frowned. "Luckily, not too much damage has been done. You can just trim the smudge off the bottom. But I'm very disappointed in you two," she said, fixing Kai and Coralie with a stern look. "If there's any more nonsense like this, you will most certainly not be coming on the camping trip. Do I make myself clear?"

Coralie and Kai opened their mouths to protest, but Ms. Sylvie shook her head. "No. I don't want to hear excuses. This is not the sort of behavior I expect from you."

She swam back to the front of the classroom.

Glenda turned to Jazeela and Racquel with a smirk.

"I can't believe Glenda!" Marina fumed when class ended and they swam out of school for the day.

"She's as mean as a stonefish!" said Kai.

"And as ugly as one!" added Coralie.

"I'm glad it's almost the weekend and we don't have to see her until Monday. You'd both better be careful from now on," said Naya anxiously. "If she gets you into any more trouble, you might not be allowed to come camping."

"I can't wait to see Melly and tell her about the trip!" said Luna. Melly was her gentle pet manatee. She had wide dark eyes that twinkled with kindness.

All five of their pets were waiting eagerly at the school gates. Along with Melly there was Sammy, Marina's tiny golden yellow seahorse; Dash, Coralie's super-speedy young bottlenose dolphin; Tommy, Kai's intelligent hawksbill sea turtle; and Octavia, Naya's clever, and often very mischievous, octopus. They were all thrilled to see the merchildren. Sammy nuzzled Marina's cheek with his tiny snout, Melly cuddled up to Luna, Dash and Tommy zoomed around Coralie and Kai in excited circles, and Octavia wrapped her eight arms around Naya's neck and gave her a hug.

Talking over each other in their excitement, the group told the pets about the trip. The creatures couldn't reply, but they did understand everything that was said to them. Dash whistled and Tommy and Melly waggled their flippers, while Sammy did somersaults and Octavia waved her arms excitedly.

"This trip is going to be so much fun!" said Luna.

"*Fin-tastic* fun!" said Coralie.

"We have to win the prize for the best project," said Marina. "So we get first choice of a camping spot!"

Coralie checked to see that there was no one close enough to listen in. "Have you finished the *you-know-whats* yet, Kai?"

"Not quite," Kai said. He had come up with the idea of making models of the three zones of the ocean to display in front of their poster. Each zone—the Sunlit Zone near the surface, the Twilight Zone farther down, and the Midnight Zone way down deep in the ocean—had different coral formations.

"I've done the Sunlit Zone and the Twilight Zone because I know what both of those look like," Kai said. "I've started the Midnight Zone—well, I've painted the inside of the driftwood box I made black—but I don't really

21

know what to put in it."

The merpeople rarely went to the Midnight Zone. It was pitch-black and home to strange creatures that had large fangs and poisonous tentacles. Sea monsters were rumored to lurk in its caves, and there were stories of merpeople who had dived down there and never returned.

"Do you have any ideas, Naya?" Kai went on.

Naya frowned. She knew a lot about most of the ocean, but very little about the Midnight Zone. "Not really. The trouble is that there's almost nothing written about it. Do you think your dad might know anything useful, Marina? Could we ask him?"

"I think he has been down to the Midnight Zone a few times to do research," said Marina. "Why don't we see if he can help? He'll be out on the deep-water reef. At breakfast, he was telling me he's doing some research on the strawberry squid that live there. They seem to be disappearing from the reef."

"Disappearing?" echoed Naya. "That doesn't sound good. Maybe we should help him investigate."

"Yes," said Kai, flicking his tail. "Save the Sea Creatures Club to the rescue!"

The five of them loved sea creatures so much that they had formed a club. They made sure they had safe places to lay their eggs and bring up their young and collected plastic litter that could be dangerous to sea creatures, and they also helped marine animals in faraway places, too—rescue missions that often ended up turning into incredible adventures.

"Let's go and find your dad," said Coralie eagerly. "I love going to the deep reef—it's so exciting! You never know what will come out of the shadows."

"And while we're there, Dash and Melly can see if they can stay underwater for longer now," said Naya. The group was always exploring and having adventures, but they had to be careful about staying underwater too long because Dash and Melly were marine mammals. That meant that they had to go to the surface to breathe oxygen every twenty minutes or so.

After a scary mission where it had looked like they were going to be trapped underwater for a long period of time, Naya had suggested that the two animals build up their ability to stay underwater for longer. She thought they could do this by increasing the length of their dives little by little and had devised a training plan. She also made an iron tonic that she was feeding to them every day. Iron helped the blood hold oxygen for longer and carry it around the body more efficiently, so Naya was hoping that her tonic would make it easier for Dash and Melly to dive for longer periods of time. They'd been taking the tonic and following her training program for two weeks now, so she was eager to see if her ideas were making a difference.

The friends set off through the sunny turquoise water, weaving around the brightly-colored coral, vase sponges big enough to fit a mermaid inside, and clusters of pink-and-white, flower-like anemones. They stopped briefly at the Marine Sanctuary where Erin, Luna's mom, worked. Being younger than the others, Luna had to check that it was okay to go out to the deep reef.

"That's fine. Just be back by dinnertime," said Luna's mom. She was exercizing an orphaned dolphin. At the sanctuary, she helped injured sea creatures and then released them back into the wild. However, orphaned babies usually couldn't be released because it would be too dangerous for them on the reef without a parent, so they were found homes with the merpeople. "And no trying to befriend dangerous creatures down there," she added. "We don't need a poisonous blue-ringed octopus or a stingray following you home, Luna!"

Luna only had to hum, and any sea creature would come to her. She could soothe even the most scared animal. It was a really useful talent for a member of the Save the Sea Creatures Club!

"All right, I'll try not to attract anything dangerous," Luna told her mom with a grin as the baby dolphin swam up and nuzzled her.

"You're so cute, little Bubbles!" she told him, kissing his head. "Mom will find you a home soon."

Coralie grinned. "I have a new dolphin joke, everyone. How does a pod of dolphins decide who should go first in a game?"

"How?" asked Luna's mom.

"They *flipper-coin*!" Coralie giggled, pointing at Bubbles' flippers.

Luna's mom shook her head. "Oh, Coralie, your jokes get worse and worse!" She turned to Naya. "Now, Naya, I've been meaning to ask you—do you have any more of those dolphin toys you made?"

"Yes! I can bring you one later," said Naya. She loved inventing, and one of the things she had dreamed up recently was a toy made from a large clamshell with holes cut in it. You could put treats inside and lock it shut. Then, when the dolphin played with the toy, the treats fell out. It kept the young dolphins

27

amused when Luna's mom was busy taking care of the other animals.

"Thank you. It would be great for Bubbles. Dolphins are so clever—they're much happier when they're kept busy."

Octavia zoomed over and pointed at herself.

Luna's mom laughed. "Yes, okay, Octavia. Octopuses are *just* as clever as dolphins."

Octavia folded her arms, annoyed, and glared at Luna's mom.

"All right, some octopuses are *even more clever* than dolphins!" Luna's mom corrected herself.

Octavia danced in the water, looking very happy.

28

"Don't worry, Dash," said Coralie, patting her dolphin. "She's just—" she looked at the others, her eyes sparkling—"*squid-ing*!"

They groaned and splashed her, but Dash clapped his flippers together and opened his mouth in a big dolphin grin, making a whistling sound. "At least Dash thinks I'm funny!" Coralie said.

"Come on—we'd better get going," said Marina.

"Yes, please take Coralie away before she tells any more jokes!" said Luna's mom, shaking her head again and smiling.

They swam on, heading for Mermaids Rock. It was a huge, submerged rock that was shaped just like a mermaid's tail. A magic whirlpool swirled at its base, and its foaming waters could transport the merpeople to any ocean in the world. All they had to do was touch the rock and say where they wanted to go. The rock also marked the entrance to the

29

shallow-water reef that was the merpeople's realm, and that day, two merguards with tridents were swimming beside it, keeping a lookout for any potential threat to the reef, like orcas.

One of the guards was Kai's mom, Indra. "Where are you off to?" she called.

Kai swam over. "To see Marina's dad in the deep reef."

"Okay, but be careful out there," his mom warned.

"We will be! See you back at home, Mom!" called Kai, and then he joined the others and they sped on toward the shadowy reef.

Chapter Three
The Mysterious Light

The deep-water reef was in the Twilight Zone—much farther down in the ocean than the shallow, sunny reef where the merpeople lived. There were caves with tunnels inside that led all the way down to the Midnight Zone, and then even farther down to the deepest reaches of the ocean—the freezing trenches of the Abyss.

As Naya and the others swam deeper, the water got colder and colder, changing from light turquoise to dark blue and finally to gray. At last, they reached a gloomy world of stony coral, with crevasses, caves, and forests of sea firs. Red arrow crabs with thin, spider-like legs crawled over the pale coral, searching for feather duster worms to eat, while bell-shaped, translucent sea jellies with long, stinging tentacles floated silently past, the inside of their bodies glowing with strands of rainbow-colored lights.

Naya shivered. She was used to visiting the deep-water reef now, but it always felt spooky and strange. She did like seeing the different creatures, though—the shoals of shining lanternfish, the gentle angel sharks, and the flat rays that swept along the rocky bottom. A snipe eel slithered past them, its slender body twisting through the water.

Coralie nudged Naya. "What did the baby eel say to the mommy eel after he'd been sick?"

"What?" said Naya.

"Please don't make me go to school—I'm not *eel-ing* well!" Coralie grinned and dodged as Naya flicked at her with her tail fluke.

They swam on through the strange, shadowy world, swerving around the sea jellies' stinging tentacles and avoiding the spines of the sea urchins on the ocean floor as they searched for Marina's dad.

"It seems quieter down here than usual," Luna said. "There aren't as many creatures."

"You're right," said Marina. "It's always pretty creepy here, but I've never known it to be quite so still."

Naya glanced at Dash and Melly, wondering how they were coping with being down so deep, but they both looked perfectly at ease. Dash was bending in and out of a row of sea sponges, and Melly was saying hello to a pair of spotted slipper lobsters. Neither of them had been back to the surface for air once. Naya felt a flutter of happiness. She loved it when her ideas worked out.

They stopped at a cave. On another adventure, they had discovered a coelacanth there—a very rare, large, armored fish.

Swimming into the cave, they peeked into the hidden crevice where the creature lived. The coelacanth was resting in the dark. She was as big as Luna, with eight fins and a body covered with hard blue scales that looked very different from the fragile scales on the merpeople's tails.

"Her babies are gone," said Naya softly. "They must have been old enough to leave her."

The coelacanth opened her eyes and gave them a wary look. Luna started to hum and swam up to her. The coelacanth relaxed, and Luna lightly petted her. The coelacanth nodded and shut her eyes again, going back to sleep.

Luna gave her a gentle kiss and swam out. "She seems fine."

Kai pointed to a large tunnel at the back of the main cave. "Do you remember the megacoelacanthus who came up through that tunnel?"

"How could we ever forget Stanley?" said Coralie. "He was ginormous!"

The megacoelacanthus was a huge version of the coelacanth. Megacoelacanthuses had been around since the time of the dinosaurs. The merpeople had thought they were extinct, but one had found its way through the tunnels that led from the Abyss and had swum into the deep reef, trying to find its way home.

Luna swam over to the tunnel mouth and frowned. "Hey, this is weird. Come and look! There's a strange light in the tunnel."

Her friends joined her. Instead of the tunnel being pitch-black, there was a light coming from farther down. It flashed on and off.

"I wonder what that is," said Kai. "Naya? Any ideas?"

"No," said Naya, puzzled. "It should be completely dark down there."

"Could it be bioluminescent plankton?" Marina asked thoughtfully.

"No, they usually have a softer, bluer glow, and they don't flash like that," said Naya. Octavia started swimming curiously toward the flashing light. Naya grabbed one of her arms. "What are you doing, Octavia? You'll end up in the Midnight Zone if you go down there."

A voice coming from the main entrance to the cave made them swing around. "Hello, everyone." It was Mr. Silverfin, Marina's dad. He had a collecting bag slung across his body and was holding a pot that glowed with green mermaid fire—a magical fire that could burn even underwater and could be used to make mermaid powder. "What are you doing down here? Why aren't you at school?"

"School finished a while ago, Dad," said Marina, shaking her head in exasperation. Her dad often lost track of time when he was working. Marina had learned to be very independent and look after herself, although she never seemed to mind.

"Oh, right," Marina's dad said. "So, why are you down here?"

"We were looking for you," said Marina. "We wanted to ask you a question about the Midnight Zone."

Her dad looked worried. "You're not thinking of going down there, are you? It's very dangerous."

"We just want to know what it's like," said Naya. "There's not much in any of my books about it, and we need to know what kind of coral grows there for our school project."

"A lot of the coral there is dead," said Marina's dad. "It falls into the Midnight Zone from the upper reaches of the sea. But you do get different kinds of stony coral and *Lophelia*, a white coral that forms dense thickets."

"How many times have you been down there?" Kai asked eagerly.

"Only a few," said Marina's dad. "Some very

vicious creatures like frilled sharks, gulper eels, and giant squid live down there, and they'll eat anything that moves. There are also very poisonous sea jellies and fish with incredibly sharp teeth. You need eyes and ears trained in all directions to stay safe, so it's too dangerous for me to go there on my own. It's a shame, because it would be very easy to get to by swimming down that tunnel."

"There's a strange light inside the tunnel today," said Marina.

Her dad frowned. "Really?" He went over and peered in. "I can't see anything."

They joined him, but he was right. The flashing light was gone, and the tunnel was just the same deep, inky black as usual.

"There was a light just a few minutes ago," said Marina. "We definitely saw it. It was flashing on and off."

Her dad scratched his chin. "Hmm. There's definitely something strange going on in these caves at the moment. I wish I knew what it was."

"What do you mean?" asked Naya, intrigued.

"The strawberry squid are vanishing," said Marina's dad, "and I don't know why."

"You mentioned that at breakfast," said Marina. "I wonder what's happening to them."

"I'll have to keep investigating," said her dad. "Speaking of which, I'd better get going. I'll see you back at the cave later, Marina."

"'Bye, Dad!" she called as he swam off.

"I hope he figures out what's going on with those squid," said Naya. Strawberry squid were tiny, bright-red squid with marks all over them that made them look like strawberries. They were very gentle and trusting.

"We need to try to help him solve the mystery. This is definitely a job for the Save the Sea Creatures Club!" said Kai.

"It is, but not for today," said Coralie reluctantly. "Aunt Erin wanted Luna to be home for dinner. We could always come back tomorrow or Sunday, though, and see if we can help figure out what's going on."

"We also need to finish our project this weekend," Naya reminded them. "I'm going to do some research and find a few pictures of stony coral, and then maybe you can make models of them, Kai?"

He nodded, and they swam to the cave entrance. Naya realized that Marina had swum back to the tunnel and was gazing inside it. "Are you coming, Marina?"

Marina's eyes shone. "You know something, I just got an idea."

Naya recognized that look. It meant Marina had thought of an adventure they could have. "What?" she said, feeling excitement fizz in her tummy. Marina usually had the best ideas!

A grin tugged at Marina's mouth. "How about we do some *real* research and go down to the Midnight Zone!"

Chapter Four
Incredible Inventions

Everyone stared at Marina, and then they all started talking at once.

"We can't go to the Midnight Zone!" Luna exclaimed.

"It would be so awesome to go," Coralie said.

Kai nodded. "It really would!"

"It's too dangerous," Naya protested. "That's what your dad said, Marina."

"No, what he actually said was that it's too dangerous to go *on his own*," Marina pointed out. "He said that you need to have eyes and ears all around. Well, if we all went, we'd be able to keep a lookout—the pets, too." She looked at them, her face full of excitement. "I'm not saying we stay down there for long, just that we go down the tunnel, take a quick look, and then come back. If we see anything scary, we'll swim right home."

"I think we should do it!" said Coralie eagerly. "Imagine how *krill-iant* it would be to actually see the Midnight Zone for ourselves."

"It would definitely help with making our model," said Kai.

"And maybe we'd also be able to solve the mystery of that flashing light we saw and discover where the disappearing strawberry squid have gone," said Marina. She turned to Naya. "Oh, come on. I know you want to see it as much as the rest of us do. Say yes, *pleeeease!*"

Naya grinned. Marina was right—she
really did want to go. "All right. I do want to
so … yes!" She glanced at Luna and saw the
younger mergirl's eyes were wide and anxious.
"But Luna, don't worry if you'd rather not
come. It's fine if you want to stay home.
We can tell you about it when we get back."

"No!" Luna said bravely, lifting her chin.
"If you're all going, I am, too. And I want
to help figure out what's happening to the

46

strawberry squid. Maybe something is coming up through the tunnels and scaring them so they're all hiding."

Or maybe something is coming up here and eating them, thought Naya, but she didn't want to upset or scare Luna, so she kept that thought to herself!

Marina cheered. "We're going on another adventure!"

"When should we go?" demanded Kai.

"Tomorrow!" Marina said. "It's Saturday, so it's perfect timing. You can ask your parents if it's okay for you to spend the day with me and then sleep over at my house. I'll borrow one of Dad's maps of the tunnels. If we meet up in the morning, then we can come here and go down to the Midnight Zone. Dad won't think to check on us—he never does when he's busy with his research. Then when we get home that night, we can finish the Midnight Zone model and have a fun sleepover. What do you say? Is it a plan?"

"It is!" they cried, high-fiving each other.

They went off to their own homes, agreeing to
meet up the next morning with anything they
thought might be useful for their Midnight
Zone adventure.

When Naya got back to the cave where she
lived with her mom, dad, and baby brother,
she headed for her bedroom. There was a large
central area in the cave with comfortable chairs
made out of squishy sea sponges in the middle
and bedrooms in smaller caves that led off the
main space, screened off by shell curtains.

Naya's bedroom had a workbench that ran
all the way along one wall. She used it for
doing experiments and creating her inventions.
Tools and science equipment hung neatly
behind it. There was a shelf filled with her

science books and a display of some of her inventions that she was particularly proud of—a treat toy, a sea-dragon hatching box, growing potion, hand warmers made from clamshells, an emergency lantern, and a bottle of iron tonic.

On the bench itself was the current invention she was working on—an ink-erasing paste to clear up octopus ink. Octavia—like most octopuses and squid—could shoot out a cloud of dark ink if she wanted to get away without anyone being able to see her. Unfortunately, she often did it when Naya's mom was scolding her, leaving ink stains all over the furniture in the cave! Naya had been trying to develop a mixture to clean them up. She'd almost managed it, but the paste always left a yellow mark behind.

Maybe it needs more salt, she thought. *And I'll try adding a spoonful of dried blue-green algae—that might get rid of the yellow.*

She got to work, adjusting the paste mixture and testing it over and over again on some inkblots Octavia made for her on a piece of sea parchment. Octavia helped by carrying ingredients to her and unscrewing bottles and jars—it was very useful having an assistant with eight arms!

Naya hummed as she worked. She always felt happiest when she was busy with an invention. She loved finding solutions to problems and seeing what happened when she combined ingredients. Doing one thing usually led to something else happening— actions caused reactions! It was one of the things she loved most about science. You could learn *why* things happened and *how* to make them happen.

Cause and effect, she thought as she painted the paste onto a large inkblot and watched as it faded and vanished. She smiled when she saw that the paper now looked as good as new.

"That's it!" she exclaimed, feeling a rush of triumph. "Look, Octavia. It's working at last."

Octavia did a victory dance, her arms wiggling up and down through the water.

Naya grinned. "Thanks for your help."

Octavia tilted the tips of her arms up—her equivalent of a thumbs up.

Naya screwed the lid on the bottle of paste and put it in her seaweed bag so she could show the others. "Okay, I'd better get the things we'll need for our adventure tomorrow."

She packed a hairbrush and toothbrush for the sleepover at Marina's, plus a new bottle of iron tonic, some test tubes, collecting jars, and a magnifying glass, as well as sharp scissors, just in case they needed to cut anything. Finally, she took five empty jars and made them into emergency lanterns. She had first made the lanterns when they had been visiting a gloomy kelp forest. She'd discovered that if she added mermaid powder to a liquid made from bioluminescent plankton and shook them together, a chemical reaction occurred that gave off light. The lanterns she'd originally made only lasted for about half an hour, but since then, she'd refined the ingredients, mixing in ground sea pansy, and now they could glow for several hours.

She got to work pouring the liquid into the jars and carefully placing sachets of mermaid powder on top. It was important that the ingredients didn't mix with each other until the lanterns were needed.

"These should be really useful in the Midnight Zone. It'll be too dark to see anything without light," she told Octavia. "But one thing I'm worried about is whether the light in the lanterns will be strong enough—it'll be pitch-black that far down."

Octavia scratched her head and then zoomed over to the jar where Naya kept the sachets of mermaid powder. Picking one up, she waved it at Naya.

"What are you trying to say?" Naya asked her.

Octavia swam over and mimed adding it to the lantern Naya was holding and then covered her eyes.

"You think that if I add more mermaid

powder, the light will be brighter?" Naya said.

Octavia nodded.

"Okay, let's see," said Naya. She unscrewed the lantern, added the extra sachet of powder, put the lid back on, and then shook the jar hard. Sparks of light flew around inside and then the liquid ignited, giving off a strong white light. It was definitely brighter than it would have been with just one sachet of mermaid powder.

"You're so clever!" Naya praised Octavia. "That's much better!"

Octavia puffed herself out proudly, then swam in front of the light. She waved her arms, making a shadow octopus appear on the white wall behind her. She swam closer to the lantern, which made her shadow grow.

"You look like a giant octopus now!" giggled Naya. Octavia threw her arms above her head and made the giant shadow octopus look like it was about to attack.

"What's going on, Naya? What's that
light?" Naya's dad had poked his head around
the shell curtain. "Oh my goodness!" he
shouted, seeing the giant shadow of Octavia.

"It's okay, Dad. It's just Octavia," said Naya,
grinning.

The alarm on her dad's face cleared as
he saw Octavia in front of the lantern and
realized what was going on. "I thought it was a
real sea monster for a minute!"

Octavia chuckled mischievously, her arms covering her mouth as her body shook.

"Octavia just had a wonderful idea about how to make my lanterns brighter," Naya told her dad.

Her dad smiled. "You two really do make a great team. However, dinner will be ready soon, and I could use some help. Can you clean up now and come and help, both of you?"

"Of course," said Naya.

Her dad swam back into the main living space.

While Octavia cleaned up the workbench, Naya finished off the lanterns, adding the extra sachet of powder to each one so they would have plenty of light when they went exploring. Excitement tingled through her at the thought of the adventure they were going to have the next day. She couldn't wait to see what they would discover in the Midnight Zone....

Chapter Five
The Adventure Begins

That night, Naya dreamed that she and the Save the Sea Creatures Club were in the Midnight Zone. They were being chased by a gigantic purple sea monster with sharp teeth and tentacles covered with huge suckers. It was following the light from their mermaid fire lanterns, its long tentacles reaching out to grab at their tails as they tried to dodge out of its way. It was getting closer and closer, its horrible jaws widening....

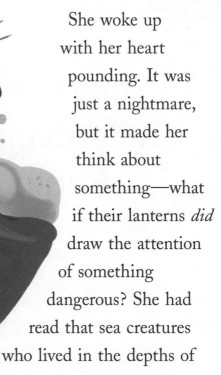

She woke up with her heart pounding. It was just a nightmare, but it made her think about something—what if their lanterns *did* draw the attention of something dangerous? She had read that sea creatures who lived in the depths of the ocean were often attracted to light. It was why some of them, like anglerfish and hatchetfish, could make parts of themselves shine and glow. They did it to tempt prey to swim to them so they could gobble it up.

It would be better if we could turn the lanterns off if we need to, Naya thought. *But how?*

She considered the problem. There was

no way of stopping the reaction once it had started—light would keep being produced until the mixture ran out. But was there a way to cover the lanterns and block the light? An idea formed in her head, and she bent over to tickle Octavia, who was asleep at the end of Naya's bed.

"I need your help, Octavia."

Octavia stretched all eight arms, yawned, and followed her over to the workbench. Naya opened a box that was full of ribbon seaweed and found four pairs of long needles made from fish bones. "I need you to do some knitting!"

Olivia was excellent at knitting—her eight arms worked at once! In next to no time, she had made five lantern covers out of the seaweed.

"Perfect!" said Naya happily. She put one over a lantern. "Now, if the light attracts any dangerous creatures, we can block it out."

Octavia shivered and wrapped her arms around herself.

"I know—hopefully we won't need to," Naya said. "But it's always best to be prepared."

Just then, she heard her mom calling her. "Naya! Marina and Kai are here!"

Naya blinked. She'd been so caught up in making the lantern covers that she had completely lost track of time. She hadn't even had breakfast yet. "Coming!"

Slinging her heavy seaweed bag across her body and picking up the lanterns by their handles, she swam out of her room.

Her mom was feeding Naya's baby brother, Orin, in the kitchen. Marina and Kai were waiting just inside the cave. Marina looked like she was going to burst with excitement. "There you are, Naya," she called as if they'd been waiting all day. "Let's go!"

"I'll see you tomorrow, Mom," Naya said.

"You haven't eaten anything," her mom protested.

Naya swam to the kitchen cupboard and

took out a handful of seaweed crackers and a couple of sea plums. "I'll take these with me."

"All right, have fun today," said her mom.

"We will!" Naya said, grinning to herself as she thought about what they were planning to do. She kissed her mom, said good-bye to Orin, and then set off with the others, eating her breakfast on the way. They stopped to pick up Coralie and Luna, and then dropped their sleepover things into Marina and her dad's cave.

"I have some candy," said Coralie, pulling a very large, multicolored glass jar out of her bag that was filled with peppermint candy. "Should I leave them here or bring them?"

"Bring them," decided Marina. "We can eat them while we're out—we might get hungry. I've packed some seaweed cookies, too. Now I just need to get Dad's map."

She swam into the cave that was her dad's study and returned a few minutes later with a huge, rolled-up map made of white sea parchment. It had a strap attached to it so it could be carried easily.

"That's enormous!" said Kai.

"I know," said Marina. She slung it over her back. "But it's the best one. It has all of the tunnels marked on it, and we might need it if we get lost."

"Oh, I hope we don't," said Luna anxiously.

"We'll be fine," Coralie reassured her.

"And who knows what amazing things we'll see," said Naya. "Hatchetfish, vampire squid, dumbo octopuses...."

"Ha! Joke time! What did the barnacle say to the octopus it was clinging on to?" Coralie interrupted.

"What?" said Naya.

"You can't get *squid* of me!" said Coralie. They all rolled their eyes, but she just grinned. "I have a ton more octopus jokes for you."

"No! Save us!" said Kai. "More of your jokes would *fin-ish* me off!"

Coralie chuckled. "*Ink* you're funny, do you, Kai?"

They high-fived.

"Enough, you two!" Naya said, shaking her head at them. "Now I have something for everyone." She gave out the emergency lanterns and explained how the covers were to be used if they wanted to block the light from shining out. "Just in case it attracts any dangerous predators," she told them. "After all, none of us wants to be an anglerfish's lunch!"

"Nice knitting, Octavia!" said Coralie, admiring the covers. Octavia looked delighted.

"This is so exciting!" said Marina, her eyes glowing. "Come on, everyone!"

As they set off, they saw Glenda swimming nearby. "What are you doing?" she said, looking suspiciously at their bulging bags.

"What does it have to do with you?" said Marina.

"Is it something to do with the project? Cos if it is, you might as well just give up," Glenda said, putting her nose in the air. "There's no way you're going to win. No way at all."

"Wait until you see our project on Monday," said Kai.

"Why? What are you planning?" Glenda demanded.

"Not telling!" said Marina.

"But it's going to be something good!" added Coralie.

"I want to know!' said Glenda. "Tell me

what you're doing."

Octavia shot a cloud of ink at Glenda. As Glenda hastily swam backward to avoid it, the group raced off as fast as they could. Glenda shouted insults after them. "You slimy eels! You brainless tubeworms!"

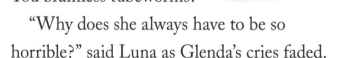

"Why does she always have to be so horrible?" said Luna as Glenda's cries faded.

Marina shook her head. "I have absolutely no idea."

"Let's not waste time talking about grumpy Glenda—let's get to the deep reef," said Coralie.

Kai cheered and swam in a circle with

Tommy. "I agree! It's time to get this adventure started!"

The tunnel gaped at them like an open mouth. When they peered inside, there was no sign of the strange flashing light that they had seen the day before. It was just very, very dark. Octavia's arms wrapped around Naya.

"I'll lead the way—you all follow me," Marina instructed. "It's probably a good idea for us to use just one lantern at a time because we don't know how long it'll take us to swim there, take a look around, and come back. We don't want to be left without any light. We'll use mine first." She shook her lantern. As the ingredients mixed together, light sparkled out.

Naya fed Melly and Dash an extra dose of iron tonic, and then they set off down the wide tunnel. Marina went first, then Coralie and Luna, and Kai and Naya brought up the rear. Their pets swam beside them. As they descended, the walls of the tunnel began to glow with blue-green algae, and the water grew colder and colder until finally the tunnel ended, and they swam out. The ocean was an inky black that seemed to absorb the light from Marina's lantern.

"Isn't it dark and quiet down here?" whispered Naya. "I almost wish whatever was making those strange lights yesterday would appear—even if it is dangerous!"

Marina held up her lantern, but they couldn't see anything outside the circle of light it cast around them.

"It's spooky!" said Luna.

"And cold!" said Kai, shivering.

"I bought some of my dad's Fire Potion. Let's drink that," said Marina. Her dad had invented Fire Potion before he went on a trip to the freezing Arctic Ocean. If you drank it, it would keep you warm for twenty-four hours. She handed Coralie her lantern and rummaged in her bag, pulling out five little bottles filled with red liquid. She handed them out, and they pulled the lids off and drank, sharing a few drops with their pets so that they could stay warm, too.

As Naya felt the red potion fizz its way down, warmth seemed to spread through her, making her tingle from her head to the tip of her tail.

"That's better!" said Coralie in relief. The animals swam in circles, looking much happier, too.

Naya saw a glowing blue cloud drifting toward them through the dark. It seemed to be made up of pinpricks of light.

"Look, everyone!" said Luna, spotting it, too, and pointing.

They huddled together and watched as the cloud drifted past about three feet away. "It's a group of firefly squid," Naya realized, noticing that the cloud was made up of many small, glowing, eight-armed squid whose bodies were covered with dots of blue light. "It's okay. They're not dangerous."

"They might not be, but what is *that*?" Coralie cried.

Chapter Six
The Glowing Cave

A very large fish with tiny eyes and the most enormous gaping mouth appeared out of the darkness. There was a long stalk attached to its head, which had a bright, shining tip like a lantern, but the group couldn't take their eyes off its yawning open mouth and long, spiny teeth.

"An anglerfish! They eat anything! Move, everyone!" gasped Marina.

They all scattered, but the fish didn't alter its course. It swam on into the dark, without looking back at them.

"Why is it moving so slowly?" said Kai. "And why didn't it try to chase us?"

"Most creatures in the Midnight Zone move really slowly to conserve energy and some, like that anglerfish, don't swim after their prey. They rely on their prey swimming to their light so they can snap it up," said Naya, remembering what she'd read.

"I'm not sure I like it down here!" said Luna with a shiver. "It feels really dangerous."

"We need more light," said Marina, holding up her lantern and trying to peer through the darkness.

"Let's activate Luna's and Kai's lanterns now, but keep mine and Coralie's for the way home," said Naya.

Luna and Kai shook their lanterns. With three, they could see their surroundings better. Like Marina's dad had said, the Midnight Zone had huge mounds of gray coral and

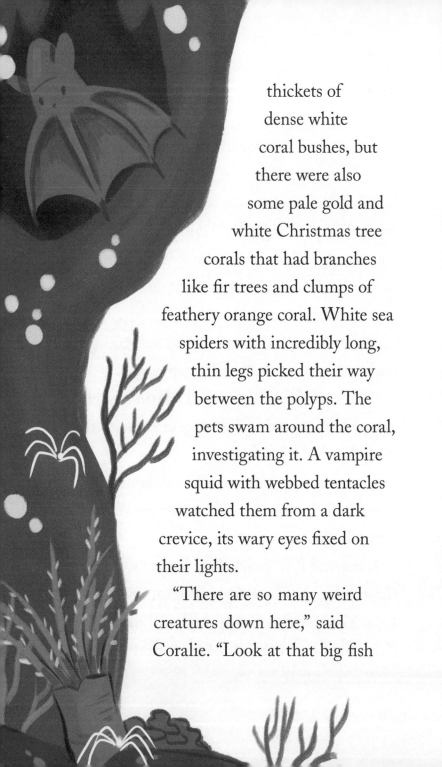

thickets of
dense white
coral bushes, but
there were also
some pale gold and
white Christmas tree
corals that had branches
like fir trees and clumps of
feathery orange coral. White sea
spiders with incredibly long,
thin legs picked their way
between the polyps. The
pets swam around the coral,
investigating it. A vampire
squid with webbed tentacles
watched them from a dark
crevice, its wary eyes fixed on
their lights.

"There are so many weird
creatures down here," said
Coralie. "Look at that big fish

over there."

A large, spotted fish with enormous green eyes and a long, thin tail was hiding behind a cluster of giant tubeworms with red tips. Sammy bobbed over to it inquisitively. As he got close, the fish lunged out from its hiding place, its jaws snapping.

"Sammy!" gasped Marina.

The little seahorse dodged just in time. He raced back to Marina and hid in her hair, his eyes wide, his tail trembling. The rattail fish retreated into the tubeworms.

"It's okay," Marina soothed Sammy, petting him with her finger.

Light suddenly flashed out in the distance. There was one long flash followed by several shorter ones.

"What's that?" said Coralie.

"It looks just like that light in the tunnel yesterday," said Luna.

The flashing-light pattern repeated itself.

"It's coming from over there," said Marina, pointing to a large cave in a hill of dead coral.

Naya realized that Octavia wasn't beside her anymore. The octopus was swimming toward the open mouth of the cave, her arms trailing out behind her, her dark eyes fixed on the flashing lights.

"Octavia! Where are you going?" cried Naya.

With a flick of her tail, she raced after the octopus and swam in front of her, stopping her in her tracks. Octavia blinked and shook her head as if to clear it.

74

"Why was Octavia swimming toward the cave?" asked Luna.

"I don't know," said Naya uneasily as Octavia tried to peer around her. "She can't seem to stop looking at those lights." She held Octavia tightly. She didn't want her pet swimming into the cave on her own. There could be something awful inside!

"Let's go and see what's in there," said Kai. As he started swimming toward the cave, a black gulper eel darted out from behind a sea fir and headed right for him. It was huge! It had a wedge-shaped head and a long, thin body with a whip-like tail. Its bottom jaw dropped open, revealing its sharp teeth and enormous jaws— definitely big enough to swallow a merboy.

"Kai!" shrieked the mergirls. Tommy had also seen what was happening. He zoomed straight at Kai, knocking him out of the way with his hard head.

"Whoa!" Kai yelled as he windmilled

through the water.

For a second, Naya thought the eel was going to spin around and come back, but Marina swung her lantern at it and yelled. It gave up, snaking on its way.

"That was close!" said Marina.

"Too close," said Kai, righting himself and swimming over to the group, holding onto Tommy's shell. His voice was shaky for the first time. "This place is seriously creepy. I've changed my mind about exploring. Why don't we go home?"

"Good plan!" agreed Coralie. "After all, we don't know how long Dash and Melly will be able to stay this deep even with Naya's tonic."

"But what about the flashing light?" said Marina. "If we don't take a look in that cave, we might never find out what's causing it."

Naya was torn between wanting to investigate and longing to get back to safety. "Marina's right. We could just take a quick look. Dash and Melly have stayed underwater for longer than this before. I'm sure they'll be fine—"

She broke off as Octavia struggled in her arms, trying to get free. "No, Octavia. I know you like those lights, but you can't go in the cave on your own. We'll all go together."

Octavia shook her head impatiently and pointed with two of her arms that she had managed to wriggle free.

Naya followed her gaze and saw an orange-and-white octopus swimming toward the cave. It had short, stubby arms and fins on top of its head that looked like large, flapping ears. "A dumbo octopus!" she said. "I've only ever seen one in a book."

"It's really cute!" exclaimed Luna.

"They're some of the deepest dwelling octopuses," said Naya.

"Maybe it lives in that cave with the lights," Luna suggested.

Naya frowned. "I don't think so. Octopuses are attracted to light, but they usually live in dark places. There might be something in the cave that's trying to lure it in using light, though."

"So the octopus could be in danger?" said Luna in alarm. The dumbo octopus was almost at the cave entrance. She raced after it, holding up her lantern. "No, little octopus! Don't go in there—it could be dangerous. Wait!"

"Luna! Be careful!" gasped Marina as Luna pushed the dumbo octopus away from the cave entrance.

Naya could hardly believe what happened next. Two enormously long tentacles covered in hundreds of large, powerful suckers suddenly shot out from the cave and wrapped around Luna's body! She shrieked and tried to swim backward, but it was too late. Before anyone could move, she was pulled

toward the cave and then, with a
scream, she disappeared inside!

Chapter Seven
A New Friend

"Luna!" Marina yelled in horror as they stared at the empty space in the water where Luna had been swimming just a few seconds before.

Coralie shot past Marina and Naya with Dash beside her. "Luna! Don't worry! I'm coming to save you!"

"Wait, Coralie!" Naya grabbed the end of Coralie's tail to slow her down. "We don't know what's in there."

Coralie struggled, trying to break free.

"Let me go, Naya! Luna's in trouble—we have to help her."

"I know we do, but let's go and look together, very carefully and very quietly. We need to find out what we're dealing with, not just go racing in." Naya's heart was pounding painfully in her chest. She also felt like rushing right into the cave, but she knew that if they all got themselves caught, that wouldn't help Luna.

Luna's voice floated faintly out of the cave. "Don't come in."

Relief flooded through Naya. Luna didn't sound like she was hurt!

"Come on," Marina hissed to the others. "Let's go and look. But quietly!"

They swam cautiously to the cave entrance and peered around its stone edges. Naya caught her breath. Luna was in the arms of a giant orange squid. Its head and mantle were huge—about six feet long—its eight arms and two tentacles were even longer, and the ends of its arms were flashing with light. Its enormous dark eyes blinked as it held Luna tightly and studied her. Then it opened its mouth and started to pull her closer.

Naya felt her blood freeze. Was it going to eat her?

Luna started to hum gently. The giant squid tipped its head to one side and paused. Luna continued humming. The squid's enormous head moved from side to side in time with the gentle tune. Its eyes grew softer. "There, see, you don't want to hurt me," Luna murmured softly. "I'm your friend. You like my song, don't you?"

She hummed some more. The squid changed its grip, turning her around in its arms until it was cradling her like a baby. One of its free arms smoothed her long hair as it rocked her from side to side and another took the lantern from her.

"Luna's magic is working," breathed Marina.

"Do you think it's going to let her go?" Coralie asked as the squid peered curiously at the lantern.

"It seems very interested in the light," said Kai.

"Squid are attracted to light, just like octopuses," said Naya.

The squid moved the light from side to

side and then placed it on a ledge beside it, where there were some small lanternfish with glowing green sides. It then moved Luna to the back of the cave.

"Why has it put her over there?" said Kai.

"I think it wants to keep me as a pet!" Luna called.

A group of dark-red strawberry squid came creeping out from nooks and crannies at the back of the cave along with several dumbo octopuses, a vampire squid, and some small lanternfish. The strawberry squid propelled themselves through the water to Luna and swam onto her lap and into her arms. They all looked scared.

Naya bit her lip and grabbed Marina's arm. "Those strawberry squid wouldn't usually live as far down in the ocean as this. They've probably come from the Twilight Zone," she whispered. "I bet the giant squid has been swimming up the tunnel and using its bioluminescence—the flashing lights at the tip of its arms—to lure them down here, then keeping them until it's hungry."

"If that's its food supply, do you think it's planning to eat Luna?" Coralie whispered back.

They exchanged horrified glances.

"Luna!" Coralie called softly. "Try to swim over to us, but move slowly so you don't alarm it."

"And hum!" said Kai. "It seems to like that."

Starting to hum again, Luna gently placed the strawberry squid back on the cave floor and began to edge toward the entrance.

WHAM!

The squid's arms slapped around her again. It shook its head at her and then placed her at the back of the cave with the other creatures.

"I don't think it's going to let me go," said Luna helplessly.

"Stay there, and we'll figure out how to rescue you," said Marina.

"Start humming if it looks like it might be getting hungry," said Naya.

"It won't eat me," said Luna confidently. "It likes me."

Naya forced a smile. "Of course it does," she said, wishing she could feel as sure as Luna. She swam away from the cave entrance with the others. They huddled next to a mound of dead coral, clustering around Marina's and Kai's lights. The pets pushed close to them, Melly sending anxious looks back at the cave.

"What are we going to do?" said Kai. "We have to get Luna out of the giant squid's clutches."

"How about we wait until it leaves the cave, and then we grab her and swim home?" suggested Coralie. Dash whistled in agreement.

"We could, but octopuses and squid like their dens and only tend to leave if they're hunting or feel threatened," Marina pointed out.

Naya nodded. "Marina's right. The giant squid has plenty of food to eat in there if it gets hungry...." Octavia shivered in her arms and hid her face in Naya's neck. Naya petted her. "There's no reason for it to leave right now."

"And we can't just wait it out down here," said Marina.

Naya nodded. "Our lights won't last, and Melly and Dash need to surface to breathe."

"There's no way we can leave Luna down here alone, trapped with that squid!" Coralie said quickly.

"No way at all," agreed Marina. "How about this for a plan? Sammy and I will stay here, and the rest of you go and get the guards. They'll be able to help us distract the squid so Luna can get out."

"We probably should, but we're going to be in so much trouble," groaned Coralie.

"And what about the giant squid?" said Naya anxiously. "I bet the merguard will hurt it. You know what they're like with creatures they feel threatened by. Not your mom, Kai," she added quickly. "But Chief Razeem. He'll probably just tell the guards to harpoon it like he almost did with Stanley, the megacoelacanthus."

"No, we can't let that happen!" Marina burst out. "I know the squid has trapped Luna, and it's been luring creatures from the Twilight Zone to its cave, but it's only acting naturally. It has to find food. It's our fault that Luna got caught and is in danger. We shouldn't have come into the squid's realm. It isn't fair if it ends up being hurt because of us."

They exchanged worried looks.

"You're right," said Kai slowly. "But what can we do? We have to get Luna out of there."

"Maybe the guards will just come down and threaten it without hurting it," said Coralie hopefully. "Then it will leave its cave, and Luna can escape."

"In which case it'll probably attack the

guards, and they'll fight back," Marina pointed out. "Oh, if only another giant squid or giant octopus would come along to make it come out."

"Could we find one, maybe?" asked Coralie. "And get it to come here."

"There isn't time," said Marina, looking around at the total darkness. "It would probably take forever to find one, and then how would we even get it to come here? Luna's the one that can get sea creatures to follow her!"

Naya's eyes widened. "Wait!" she exclaimed, looking at Octavia in her arms and then at the lanterns Marina and Kai were holding. "We don't need to go hunting for a giant octopus. We have one right here!"

Naya's friends stared at her in astonishment as she pointed at Octavia. "But Naya, Octavia is not a giant octopus," said Marina slowly.

"No, but we can make her *look* like one by using our lanterns and the back of the map!" said Naya, remembering how Octavia had pretended to be a giant octopus in her bedroom. She explained her idea. "We'll need to put all the lanterns together, except mine, which we'll use to see. Octavia, can you get the lantern covers and scissors out of my bag, please, and put covers over three of the lanterns? I'll cut a hole in each one so we can direct the light where we want it to go."

She swam a little way off until she was directly opposite the cave entrance. "Marina, can you bring the map over here? I need you to unroll it and hold it up while Tommy and Dash pull down the bottom corners to keep it straight. The back of it—the plain white side—needs to be facing toward the cave entrance. It's going to be our screen."

Marina, Tommy, and Dash did as she asked.

"And you two—" Naya turned to Kai and Coralie—"can you activate the remaining lanterns and put the covers over them?"

91

While they got to work, Naya cut a hole in the front of each lantern cover to allow some light to come out. She then set the lanterns down on a flat rock near the cave entrance, angling them so they appeared black from behind, but the beams of light coming from the front of them were all trained on the white sheet. "Are you ready, Octavia?"

Octavia nodded.

"Time to be a giant octopus!" said Naya.

Coralie, Kai, and Naya hid in the shadows beside the cave entrance with Melly, who was keeping an eye on Luna, and Sammy. They watched as Octavia zoomed in front of the lights. As the beams hit her, her shadow appeared on the white map. She moved closer and closer to the lanterns, and the shadow kept on growing bigger. She looked just like a giant, menacing octopus! She lifted her arms and wriggled them, and her shadow did the same.

Naya held her breath. Would her plan work?

Chapter Eight
Escape!

"Nothing's happening," whispered Coralie.

"Wait," said Naya, hearing the faintest of noises. All of a sudden, the giant squid burst out of the cave. It threw up its arms and waved them furiously. It was staring so intently at the shadow octopus that it didn't notice Octavia near the ground, dancing in front of the light. Octavia dodged to one side, and the squid followed the shadow's movements.

"Get Luna out of the cave while the squid's busy!" Naya hissed to Coralie and Kai.

Sammy and Melly were already on it.
They zoomed into the cave. A few
seconds later, they reappeared
with Luna beside
them. But not
just Luna!
She was
shepherding
all of the
other creatures
out, too. Melly
nudged the little
strawberry squid
back toward the tunnel
with help from Kai and Coralie.
Meanwhile, the dumbo octopuses and
other Midnight Zone creatures shot away
into the safety of the shadows.

The giant squid's movements slowed down,
and it started to peer suspiciously at the screen.
Naya's heart sank. It looked like it was starting

to realize that a trick had been played on it. *If it sees Marina, Dash, Tommy, and Octavia, they'll be in real danger*, she thought. *What can I do? I need to find a way to distract it so we can all escape. But how? What do squid like?*

Looking around desperately, she caught sight of the big bottle of candy bulging out of Coralie's seaweed bag. An idea popped into her head.

"Coralie!" she hissed. "I need your jar of candy!"

To her relief, her friend didn't waste time asking why. She just pulled out the jar and handed it to Melly, who swam over to Naya with it in her mouth. "Thanks, Melly!" Naya said, tipping out the candy. Time was running out. The giant squid was reaching out its arms as if to tear the screen down.

Naya pulled the cover off of the brightest lantern and shoved the large glass jar with its multicolored squares over the top. The colorful light caught the squid's attention, and it turned in surprise. Naya dove into the cave with it, her heart pounding. She put it down on the floor, and the dark walls of the cave lit up with a colorful mosaic of light. She managed to get out of the cave just before the giant squid came zooming back in. It stared around, entranced, as it looked at the pattern of light.

"Quick, Marina! Roll the map up, and let's go through the tunnel!" gasped Naya, racing out of the cave. "And don't let those strawberry squid see the lights," she added to Coralie and Kai. The last few had spotted the colorful display and had started to drift back out of the tunnel, toward the cave.

"Oh, no, you don't," said Coralie quickly. "We're going back to the Twilight Zone. All of us." She, Kai, and Luna shooed the squid up into the tunnel again, while Marina helped Naya grab the lanterns from the ground. Naya took one last peek inside the cave. The giant squid was staring, mesmerized, at the rainbow ceiling. Its arms were waving as if it were trying to catch the light patterns, and it looked completely and wonderfully happy.

"Bye," Naya breathed to it. "Stay safe here in the Midnight Zone from now on." And then she shot into the tunnel after the others.

By the time they got back to the Twilight Zone, only two of the lanterns were still shining.

"Wow," Marina said in relief as they reached the end of the tunnel. "That is one adventure I'm not going to forget anytime soon!"

"Me, neither. That giant squid was super scary," said Kai.

"I'm glad the strawberry squid got away. The Save the Sea Creatures Club saved the day again!" said Luna.

Coralie grinned. "You know what they should have said to the giant squid as they swam away?"

"What?" said Naya.

"So long, *sucker*!" Coralie exclaimed. She grinned and nudged Kai and Naya. "Oh, come on. That was funny!"

They all started to giggle, the relief they felt at having escaped washing over them.

"What's going on here?" They jumped as Marina's dad appeared in the cave entrance. "I thought I heard voices, but you weren't here a minute ago when I swam by. And where have all these strawberry squid suddenly come from?" he said in astonishment as he looked at the school of squid milling around the cave. "Did they come up through the tunnel?"

"Yes, we found them in the Midnight Zone," admitted Marina. "A giant squid had been using its bioluminescence to lure them down there."

Her dad's forehead crinkled in a frown. "You've been down to the Midnight Zone?"

Marina nodded. "Just for a quick visit. For our school project. We didn't stay that long."

"Marina! I told you it was dangerous!" her dad exclaimed. But although he spoke crossly, a look of curiosity appeared in his eyes. "So, what did you see beside the squid? It's so quiet and still down there, isn't it? Did you see a

100

bunch of amazing creatures?"

Naya smiled to herself. If it had been any other parent, the five of them would have been in serious trouble! But although he did always try and keep Marina safe, Marina's dad understood the urge to go exploring and find things out.

"It was incredible but very scary," said Marina.

"The squid we met wanted to keep me in its cave!" Luna put in.

"But Octavia pretended to be a giant octopus and saved the day!" added Kai.

The whole story tumbled out.

Marina's dad's eyes grew wider. "Jumping jellyfish! I knew it would be dangerous down there, but I didn't expect that! You really should have listened to me—I don't want anything to happen to any of you. You mustn't go down there again, understand?"

"I'm sorry, Dad," Marina said apologetically.

Her dad shook his head in wonderment.

"I am slightly jealous, though. A giant squid…. Not many merpeople ever get to see one of those. You'll have to tell me more about it—I want to know every little detail."

Marina hugged him. "You're the best!" He looked surprised but happy.

"So the giant squid has been using its light to lure the squid into the tunnel?" said Marina's dad. "It sounds as if we'd better block the tunnel so it can't do that anymore. Then it can live its life naturally in the Midnight Zone, and the Twilight Zone's strawberry squid will be safe. And —" he fixed them with a look—"if I block off the tunnel, I'll know for sure that all of *you* won't be able to use it to go back down there again, either."

"Don't worry, Dad, we're not planning another visit anytime soon," Marina said. "It was a *clam-tastic* adventure, but I think going to the Midnight Zone once was more than enough!"

They all nodded emphatically.

Dash nudged Coralie and motioned upward with his nose. "We'd better go up to the surface," said Coralie, petting him. "Dash and Melly have managed very well after all of Naya's training, but they need to breathe some air now."

"All right. I'll see you back at home," said Marina's dad. "And no more adventures on the way, okay?"

"No more adventures," Marina repeated. "Not just yet, anyway," she added with a grin.

Chapter Nine
Sabotage

It was getting dark as they swam back to the merpeople's reef. At Marina's cave, they made themselves sandwiches and curled up on the sea-sponge cushions in the living room, around the pot of burning mermaid fire. The animals settled beside them.

"I'm so tired," yawned Coralie, smiling at a sleeping Dash.

Octavia snuggled into Naya's arms. Luna and Melly were already fast asleep. Tommy's eyes were closed, and he was snoring.

Naya took a bite of her sandwich, feeling almost too tired to eat.

"We really should go and finish the model of the Midnight Zone," said Marina, but she looked in no hurry to get up.

"Tomorrow," said Kai, glancing over at the unfinished model sitting on the table. "We can make models of the coral we saw down there as well as models of the creatures like the anglerfish, rattail fish, and the gulper eel. We can take it into school early on Monday and add it to our project so that it's ready for Ms. Sylvie to judge."

"Good plan," murmured Coralie, her eyes closing.

"Very good plan," Marina agreed, tucking her hands under her cheeks and falling asleep with Sammy curled in her hair.

Kai looked at Naya. "You and Octavia were incredible today. We might not have rescued Luna if it hadn't been for both of you."

Naya kissed Octavia's head. "Octavia was amazing. She did a wonderful impression of a fierce giant octopus!" Octavia looked very proud. "I'm just glad we all got back safely," Naya continued. Glancing over, she realized that Kai had now fallen asleep, too.

She sighed, feeling warm and content. They'd been to the Midnight Zone and made it back in one piece, she'd seen creatures she had thought she might only ever read about in books, *and* she'd helped to trick a giant squid. What a *fin-credible* adventure!

"And, after all of that, I really hope our poster wins the competition at school," she whispered to Octavia.

Octavia nudged her sleepily. Smiling happily, Naya cuddled her closer and fell asleep, too.

"What *is* Glenda doing?" Marina hissed on Monday morning as they saw Glenda heading for the school gates, looking around furtively as if she didn't want to be seen.

The group had met early that morning. The reef was very quiet as they headed to school—the other merpeople were waking up for the day, and the sea creatures were only just starting to stir. The water felt clear and cool. They had decided to get up extra early so they could add the finished models to their display. Kai was carrying them in his big driftwood crate. They looked wonderful—especially the one of the Midnight Zone that Kai had finished the day before. As well as making models of the coral, Kai had drawn pictures of the creatures they had seen and stuck them on sticks so they could be moved up and down in the display. There was even a giant squid that popped out from inside a cave!

As they got closer to school, they spotted Glenda swimming toward it with a big bag. She kept glancing around, as if checking that no one was following her.

"She looks like she's up to something," said Naya suspiciously.

"And why is she here so early?' said Marina.

"Let's hide and see what she does!" said Kai.

They ducked down behind a large clump of sea sponges and watched Glenda reach the school gates. She glanced behind her once more, then opened the gates and went inside.

Marina beckoned to everyone, and they swam silently up to the gates. Glenda was darting across the playground. The school buildings were made of elaborate multicolored coral with natural openings for windows. There were two large classrooms—one for the younger merchildren and one for the older merchildren aged seven to twelve, who were taught by Ms. Sylvie.

They watched as Glenda swam into their classroom through one of the windows.

"She's definitely up to something," hissed Marina.

"I have a bad feeling about this," said Coralie. "We'd better find out what she's doing!"

They raced to the school building, their pets at their side.

"It's lucky Ms. Sylvie isn't here yet," Naya whispered to Octavia. Pets were banned from the school grounds, and they didn't want to get in trouble before the camping trip.

Reaching the window, they peered inside and gasped.

All of the projects had been set out on the desks. Their poster was on the stand Kai had made. Glenda was swimming up to it. She had taken a giant pot of squid ink out of her bag and was unscrewing the top.

"She's planning on ruining our poster!" cried Luna.

Several things happened at once. Hearing Luna, Glenda glanced around guiltily. At the same time, Octavia used her jet propulsion to

110

zoom in through the window at top speed.
Her head thumped the pot of ink straight out
of Glenda's hand. It flew backward, the loose
lid coming off, and as it turned over, the black
contents rained down on the project on the
desk in front—Glenda, Jazeela, and Racquel's.

There was a moment of stunned silence.
Octavia's arms flew to her open mouth.

"Look what you've done, Octavia!" squeaked Glenda, staring wide-eyed at her project. "It's ruined!"

"What *Octavia's* done? You were about to ruin *our* project!" Marina exclaimed hotly, swimming in through the window. "You were going to cover it in ink!"

"You're horrible!" exclaimed Kai.

"Really mean!" shouted Coralie.

"I was only going to put a few drops on it, just to make it look a little less good so ours would win!" Glenda said, starting to cry. "Oh, I'm going to be in so much trouble."

"Well, don't expect us to feel sorry for you!" Marina said angrily. "It isn't our fault your project is ruined. You brought in the ink!"

"Wait!" interrupted Naya, diving in through the window. Despite everything, she couldn't help but feel sorry for Glenda. "Look, I think this *is* partly our fault," she said, turning to her friends. "Stop shouting and listen to me.

I know Glenda's not always very nice to us—"

"She's *never* very nice to us," Coralie muttered.

Naya ignored her. "And I know it was really mean of her to try to ruin our project," she continued, "but if we're honest, we're not always super nice to her. We tease her about stuff, like the way her porpoise behaved, and we sometimes play tricks on her. Because we do those things, it makes her want to be mean to us. In science, actions cause reactions. Doing one thing leads to something else happening. I think it's the same with people."

There was silence as everyone considered this. Glenda sniffed and looked at the floor.

Luna swam up to Naya. "Naya's right. We should be kinder." She turned to Glenda. "I'm sorry about your project, Glenda. I really am."

Glenda swallowed. "Thanks, Luna." For once, she didn't sound snooty at all. She

113

brushed her tears away. "The others are going to be so upset. We worked really hard on it. I know my dad got the coral for us, but we did everything else. And I would have gotten the coral myself, but Dad never lets me leave this reef. I've never used the whirlpool on my own, and I haven't even been to the deep reef. You're so lucky that you're able to go to so many incredible places. Especially you, Marina. You've traveled all over the world. Now I'm not even going to be allowed to go on the field trip. When Ms. Sylvie finds out what I was going to do, there's no way she'll let me come."

Marina's face relaxed, and she gave Glenda a friendlier look. "I am lucky. And I'm sorry about your project, Glenda. We … we won't tell Ms. Sylvie why you were here this morning, so don't worry about being banned from the trip."

Coralie and Kai nodded.

"And we won't tease you anymore," said Coralie.

"I really wish there was something we could do to help you fix your project," said Kai, examining the ink-splattered poster. "You did put a lot of work into it."

Octavia pulled at Naya's bag with two of her arms.

"What are you doing, Octavia?" Naya said.

Octavia opened the bag and rummaged inside. She took out a pot and a brush and waved them in the air.

"The ink eraser I made!" gasped Naya, realizing what her clever pet was trying to tell her. "Of course!" With all of the shouting, she hadn't even thought about it. Could it repair the damage?

"What is it?" said Marina as Naya took the ink eraser and brush from Octavia.

"It's a new invention I've been working on. It removes squid and octopus ink," Naya replied. "It might get the ink off your poster before Ms. Sylvie arrives," she said to Glenda. "Should I try?"

"Yes, please!" said Glenda.

Naya unscrewed the lid and used the brush to paint the paste onto the blobs of ink scattered across Glenda's poster. For a moment, nothing happened and then, before their eyes, the splotches started to shrink and disappear!

"Oh, wow," breathed Glenda. "It's working!"

"Your inventions are so awesome," Kai told Naya.

"They really are," said Glenda, sounding stunned.

"I'm afraid a few of the words have been erased, too," said Naya apologetically.

"I can easily fill those in," said Glenda. "It might look a little messy, but at least my group will have a project to hand in." She took a breath. "Thank you, Naya," she said, sounding more sincere than she ever had before. "I promise I'll never tease you about your inventions and being a geek again and I'm—I'm...." She gulped and looked around at the rest of the group. "I'm *sorry* for planning to ruin your project and for being mean. I-I hope you do win today." Her cheeks blushed as red as a strawberry squid. "I'll see you guys later—bye!" She dove through the window and dashed away.

No one spoke.

"Well, that was unexpected," Kai said slowly.

"Glenda seemed almost … nice," said Luna in astonishment.

Marina hugged Naya. "It was because of you. You were right to say what you did. In the past, she's been mean, and we've been mean, and one thing has led to another—meanness only leads to more meanness. You were kind to her just now, and she was kinder to us."

"I'm happy to make the most of having nice Glenda—while she lasts!" said Naya.

"We should get our project set up," said Kai.

"Yes, Ms. Sylvie will be here soon," added Luna.

"And then it will be competition judging time!" said Coralie in excitement.

"Oh, I really hope we win!" breathed Naya.

Chapter Ten
Camping Fun

The five merchildren watched nervously as
Ms. Sylvie swam to all of the desks, reading
the posters and examining the projects. Naya
crossed her fingers as Ms. Sylvie judged theirs.

"Excellent! I do like these displays you've
made," she said, looking impressed as she
moved the sticks in each driftwood box,
making cut-out creatures pop up in the coral.
"The information is very accurate. I also like
the original design of the whole project and
the drawings. Great job!"

The group exchanged delighted looks as Ms. Sylvie moved on to Glenda, Jazeela, and Racquel's project. She inspected it. "Well, I can see you've put a lot of work in, girls, but it is a little messy, so I'm afraid you'll have to lose a few points for that." She wrote a note on her clipboard and swam on.

At last, Ms. Sylvie was ready to announce the results.

"Here we go!" whispered Naya as she and the rest of the friends held hands.

"You've all done very well. I'm really happy with the work you put in," said Ms. Sylvie. "But the winning group for the coral project competition is...." She smiled at Naya and the others. "Naya's table!"

A week later, Marina, Kai, Coralie, Naya, and Luna were sitting at the waterline on a white sandy beach. Little waves broke over their tails in a flurry of foam, and the sun shone down out of a clear blue sky. Farther out to sea, their pets were playing tag in the crystal-clear water.

That morning, everyone in the class had used the magic whirlpool to travel to the atoll. Naya's group had been allowed to choose their camping spot first and had picked a cave on the reef, which was just a short swim from the beach. Luna had commented that the only thing wrong with it was that it didn't have a giant squid inside! They had put their seaweed sleeping bags inside it and swum back to the beach to explore. Now they were passing around the giant bag of peppermint candy that had also been part of their prize.

"It makes up for the candy we had to leave in the Midnight Zone!" said Coralie.

"Maybe the giant squid will have found them and eaten them," said Luna.

"A squid with a sweet tooth? Don't be *squid-iculous*!" said Coralie. They all groaned.

Farther along from where they were sitting, Glenda, Jazeela, and Racquel were perched at the edge of a rock pool, braiding each other's hair and making silly faces in the still water. The other merchildren were sitting on the sand or playing games in the water.

Ms. Sylvie popped up through the surface a

little way away. "Okay, everyone. Time to get going with studying the reef now that you've chosen your campsites and had a break. I'm going to give each group a quiz sheet." She held up a pile of clipboards. "I want you to try to find every coral on the sheet. First team who finds all of the different kinds of coral is the winner!"

The merchildren swam over to her, and she handed out the clipboards.

"Come on—we're going to win!" Glenda cried to Jazeela and Racquel. She looked over at Naya's group. "We're going to beat you!" But for once, her tone was playful rather than mean.

"Oh, no, you're not!" said Luna, putting her hands on her hips but smiling. "We'll beat you easily!"

Marina nudged Naya. "Someone's gotten a lot braver," she whispered.

Naya smiled. A few months ago, Luna had

been too scared to speak to Glenda and her friends, and now she was confident enough to tease them. The Save the Sea Creatures Club didn't just help sea creatures—it helped people, too!

Naya caught sight of Octavia sneaking over to Glenda's team's clipboard. She saw Octavia's arms reach out to grab it.

"No, Octavia!" said Naya, diving at her and pulling her away. "We're not going to play tricks today," she scolded her. "If we win, we're going to win fair and square!" Octavia gave her a playful look and shot away, squirting out a cloud of ink as she went. Naya dodged it just in time.

Ms. Sylvie's eyes sparkled. "Well said, Naya. I like that attitude. May the best team win!"

"That's us, of course," Marina told Glenda as they swam away.

"Nope, definitely us!" retorted Glenda with a grin.

"It's not going to be either of our groups if you two keep on arguing," Naya pointed out.

"Naya's right," said Marina as Glenda swam off with Racquel and Jazeela. "Let's get going. We have coral to find!"

"We'll need to be really fast," said Coralie.

"Um, don't you mean *reef-ly* fast, Coralie?" Kai said with a grin. He shot away, holding on to Tommy's shell. With cheers and shouts, Naya and the rest of the group followed him. Their Midnight Zone adventure might be over, but their camping fun had just begun!

Turn the page to learn more about the Midnight Zone and the creatures that live there!

THE MIDNIGHT ZONE

The Midnight Zone is the deepest region of the ocean, found at around 3,300 feet (1,000 m) below sea level. No sunlight can reach it, so there is always total darkness.

The creatures that thrive in the deep sea have adapted to survive in this harsh environment, some taking on interesting and unusual characteristics.

One creature that has adapted is the anglerfish. The females use their bioluminescent light to catch prey. Bioluminescence is light that certain kinds of fish (and other organisms) give off naturally through a chemical reaction. As it happens inside their bodies, they are able to glow even in complete darkness.

Other adaptations include protruding jaws, huge eyes, and red skin. Red skin is great camouflage, as red is the first color to become undetectable as sunlight fades.

Due to its depth, freezing temperatures, and extreme pressure, humans have only recently developed technology to make exploration of the Midnight Zone possible. There is much more to discover and many species we have yet to learn about.

ATOLLS

An atoll is a circular-shaped coral reef, island, or series of islets. An atoll surrounds a body of water, called a lagoon, and protects it from the open sea. Most of the world's atolls can be found in the Pacific and Indian Oceans.

Atolls are created when an undersea volcano continues to erupt, piling lava on the seafloor and eventually rising above the water's surface, becoming an oceanic island. Corals then start to build a reef around the island, creating a fringing reef.

Through millions of years, the volcano erodes and sinks to the seafloor, and after time, a ring-shaped coral reef is left behind, and an atoll is formed.

Atolls are some of the islands with the lowest elevation. This means that they are at risk of erosion due to waves and wind.

Sea level rise also poses a risk to atolls. As the ocean rises, atolls are flooded and may disappear.

MEET OCTAVIA
THE OCTOPUS

Octopuses have eight arms, and in each of the arms is a bundle of neurons that act as a brain! This means that each arm is capable of acting independently, while the central brain can also exert control over all of them. Each arm is lined with hundreds of suckers, allowing them to touch, smell, and manipulate objects.

There are roughly 300 species of octopus. They typically live alone, sometimes in dens

that they build from rocks, and sometimes in shells they cover themselves with. They mostly feed on crabs, shrimp, and mollusks.

Octopuses have soft bodies, meaning they can squeeze into impossibly small spaces, as long as the holes aren't smaller than their beaks—the only hard part of their bodies. They are also able to lose an arm and regrow it later.

Octopuses are amazing at camouflage! They can change both the color and texture of their skin to match their surroundings. There is even a type of octopus—the mimic octopus—that can contort its body and modify its behavior to disguise itself as animals that predators tend to avoid!

Octopuses have other methods of protection. When predators get too close, octopuses can escape by shooting themselves forward. They do this by expelling water. They are also able to release a cloud of black ink, obscuring them and dulling the predator's sense of smell.

LEARN MORE ABOUT GIANT SQUID

The giant squid is the biggest invertebrate on Earth—yet remains a mystery to scientists due to their hostile deep-sea habitat.

Giant squid are thought to grow to at least 33 feet (10 m) long. The largest giant squid that has been found was 59 feet (18 m) long and weighed almost 2,000 pounds (900 kg).

To detect objects in the total darkness of their habitat, giant squid have the largest eyes in the animal kingdom, measuring around 10 inches (25 cm) in diameter. They can be as big as a beach ball!

Giant squid have eight arms and two longer feeding tentacles, which help them bring food to their beak-like mouths.

They move their huge bodies using fins, which
seem too small for their bodies. They also use
their funnel to propel themselves forward.
They draw water into the main part of the
body, known as the mantle, and then force it
back out of the body.

DISCOVER HOW THE SAVE
THE SEA CREATURES
CLUB FIRST MADE A
SPLASH!

mermaids ROCK

The Coral Kingdom

by Linda Chapman

Illustrated by
Mirelle Ortega

1

Chapter One
The Deep-Water Reef

"Watch out, Sammy!" Marina exclaimed as a black gulper eel came swimming out of a gloomy cave with its huge mouth wide open. Sammy, her pet seahorse, zoomed out of the way just in time. With a flick of her silvery green tail, Marina flattened herself against a coral tree and watched the eel swim past. Its gaping mouth looked almost big enough to swallow her up, too, but luckily, it didn't seem interested in eating a mermaid for breakfast!

Sammy zoomed up to her shoulder, curling his golden yellow tail and hiding behind a strand of her thick brown hair. They watched the eel flick its whip-like body and disappear into the thicket of coral trees, snapping up an unlucky spider crab as it went.

Marina tickled Sammy's chest. "That was close!" Sammy butted his little head against her finger, his dark eyes shining. She kissed him, making his tiny horns wriggle in delight. He'd been her pet—and best friend—for a year now, and she couldn't bear the thought of anything bad happening to him.

"We need to be very careful down here in the deep-water reef," she warned. "There are all kinds of strange creatures around, and some of them will be dangerous. It's not like the shallow-water reefs we're used to."

Marina shifted the seaweed bag on her shoulder. She'd traveled around the oceans with her merman dad for all of her eleven years. He was a marine scientist who specialized in studying rare species, and they had been to some amazing places together—Pacific atolls, kelp forests in the Norwegian fjords, tropical coastlines.... However, this was the first deep-water reef she had visited. The water was much colder this far below the surface of the ocean. It was a gloomy world of mountains and crevasses and caves, and wherever she looked, there were mounds of gray, dead coral topped with a blanket of living purple, yellow, blue, and red coral bushes and feathery pale anemones.

Her dad had told her that some of the tunnels in the reef led to the Midnight Zone and then went even farther down to the Abyss—the deepest trenches of the ocean. It was said that some incredibly ancient sea creatures lived in the Abyss, but no one had ever been there—and returned. Marina shivered. She loved exploring, but even she didn't want to go that far down! The eerie, twilight world of the deep-water reef was exciting enough.

"I wonder where Dad is," she said to Sammy as they weaved in and out of the orange coral trees that stretched their branches up toward the surface. A shoal of large fish swam by, their fins flicking against Marina's tail as they passed, and a couple of spiny lobsters picked their way across the sandy bottom.

Marina kept her eyes open for the pot of green mermaid fire that her dad always carried with him to help him see. "I hope we find him soon," she said to Sammy. "I don't want to be late for my first day of school." Excitement curled in her tummy. School! It had been a couple of years since she and her dad had stayed long enough in one place for her to go to school, and she couldn't wait. She was really looking forward to making friends and settling down.

JOIN NAYA AND HER
FRIENDS FOR THEIR
NEXT ADVENTURE IN...

The Emerald Maze

COMING SOON!

Dive into all of the adventures in Mermaids Rock!

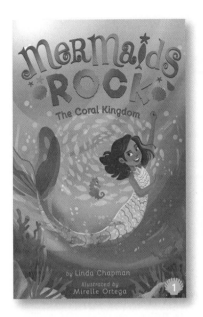

MERMAIDS ROCK
The Coral Kingdom

by Linda Chapman
Illustrated by Mirelle Ortega

1

MERMAIDS ROCK
The Floating Forest

by Linda Chapman
Illustrated by Mirelle Ortega

2

MERMAIDS ROCK
The Ice Giant

by Linda Chapman
Illustrated by Mirelle Ortega

3

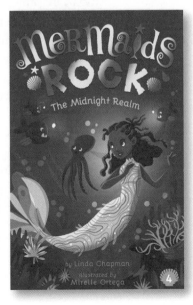

MERMAIDS ROCK
The Midnight Realm

by Linda Chapman
Illustrated by Mirelle Ortega

4

About the Author

Linda Chapman is the best-selling
author of more than 200 books. The
biggest compliment she can receive is
for a child to tell her he or she became
a reader after reading one of her books.
She lives in a cottage with a tower
in Leicestershire, England, with her
husband, three children, two dogs,
and one pony. When she's not writing,
Linda likes to ride, read, and visit
schools and libraries to talk to people
about writing.

About the Illustrator

Mirelle Ortega is a Mexican artist based
in Southern California. She grew up in the
south-east of Mexico, and developed a true
love of magic, vibrant colors, and ghost
stories. She also loves telling unique stories
with interesting characters and a touch of
magic realism.